Written and Illustrated by
Diane Madison Pitman

German School is Cool, Deutsche Schule ist Toll!

Copyright, 2019 by Diane Madison Pitman

Published by Kindle Direct Publishing

German School is Cool!

Deutsche Schule ist Toll!

Written and Illustrated by
Diane Madison Pitman

**Dedicated to all the teachers
at the Twin Cities German Immersion School**

Special Thanks to Frau Nieters
for the accurate German translation

**Gewidmet allen Lehrern der
Twin Cities German Immersion School**

Spezielles Dankeschön an Frau Nieters
für die genaue deutsche Übersetzung

Come with me to German School!
I am the school mouse.
Look for me on the pages of this book.

Komm mit mir zur Deutschen Schule!
Ich bin die Schulmaus.
Such auf den Seiten dieses Buches nach mir.

Every day we are greeted at the door
by our principal.

Jeden Tag werden wir von unserem
Schuldirektor an der Tür begrüßt

We bring our Schultütes on the first day of school.
They are filled with treats and surprises!

Am ersten Schultag bringen wir unsere Schultüten mit.
Sie sind voller Leckereien und Überraschungen!

Every boy and girl has their own locker.
Can you say the numbers you see?

Jeder Junge und jedes Mädchen
hat einen eigenen Spind.
Kannst du die Zahlen sagen, die du siehst?

one two three four five

eins zwei drei vier fünf

At the Herbstfest we celebrate Fall
with crafts, music, games and food.

Beim Herbstfest feiern wir den Herbst mit
Bastelarbeiten, Musik, Spielen und Essen.

Apple day is all about apples!
Name some things you can make with apples.

Am Apfeltag dreht sich alles um Äpfel.
Nenne einige Dinge,
die du mit Äpfeln machen kannst.

On Saint Nicholas Eve we set out our boots.
In the morning they are filled with candy and gifts.

An Sankt Nicholaus Abend ziehen wir unsere Stiefel aus.
Am morgen sind sie mit Süßigkeiten
und Geschenken gefüllt.

Field trips are always interesting.
We enjoyed this trip to the aircraft museum.

Schulreisen sind immer interessant.
Wir haben die Reise
zum Flugzeugmuseum genossen.

Kaffeeklatsch is a time for parents
to meet over coffee and German pastries.
Which one would you like to eat?

Am kaffeeklatsch treffen sich die Eltern
bei Kaffee und deutschem Gebäck.
Welches würdest du gerne Essen?

On St. Martin's Day we make lanterns.
We all walk in a parade, singing and
holding our lanterns high.

Am Sankt Martinstag machen wir Laternen.
Wir gehen alle in einer Parade und singen
und halten unsere Laternen hoch.

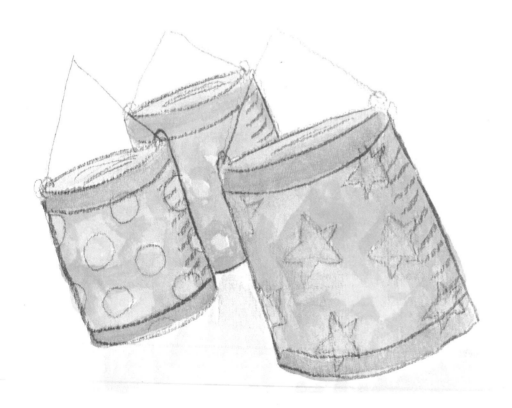

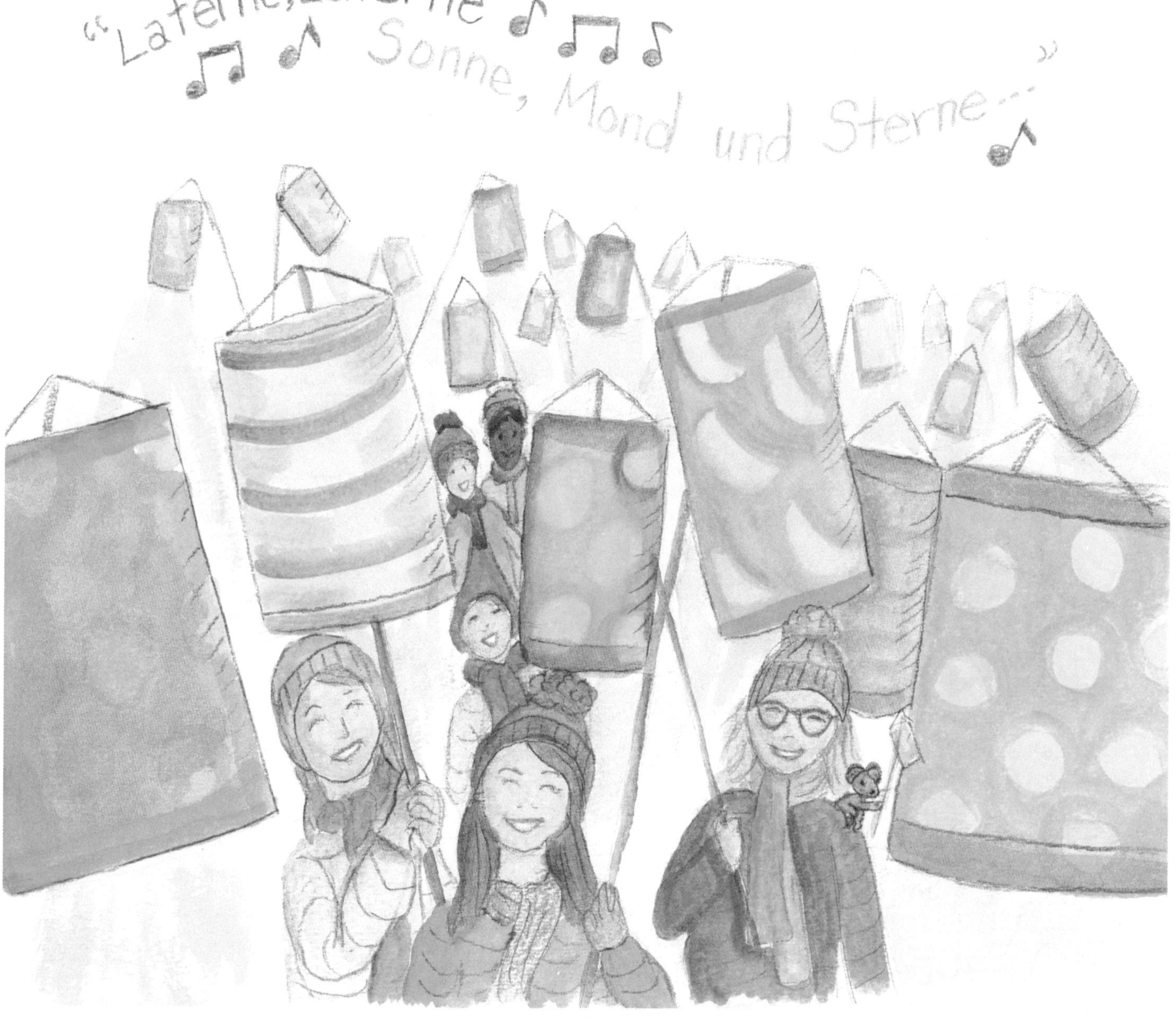
"Laterne, Laterne
Sonne, Mond und Sterne..."

At the Carnival of Cultures we learn about all
the people of the world with songs and dances.
Can you name the colors you see?

Beim Karneval der Kulteren lernen wir alle Menschen
der Welt mit Leidern und Tänzen kennen.
Kannst du die Farben nennen, die du siehst?

blau

red

gelb

green

yellow

rot

blue

grün

Field Day is where we compete in races and games.
Would you like to run with me?

Am Sporttag treten wir in Rennen und Spielen an.
Möchtest du mit mir laufen?

Thank you for joining me on the tour through my school.
You did such a great job finding me!
You have earned a Mausmünze. Goodbye!

Danke, dass du mich auf der Reise
durch meine Schule begleitet hast.
Du hast mich super gefunden!
Du hast eine Mausmünze verdient.

Auf Wiedersehen!

Made in the USA
Columbia, SC
02 February 2020

87417809R00018